Footnotes to an Unfinished Poem

Also by Stephen Berg

Bearing Weapons

The Queen's Triangle

Nothing in the Word

The Daughters

Clouded Sky by Miklós Radnóti

(with Steven Polgar and S. J. Marks)

Grief

Oedipus The King *(with Diskin Clay)*

With Akhmatova at The Black Gates

Sea Ice

In It

Bankei: First Song: 1653

Crow with No Mouth: Ikkyū

Homage to The Afterlife

New & Selected Poems

Sleeping Woman *(a public art collaboration with Tom Chimes)*

The Steel Cricket: Versions 1958-1997

Oblivion

Shaving

Porno Diva Numero Uno

Halo

Jane, this

Footnotes to an Unfinished Poem

dirty book!

Stephen Berg

Steve

ORCHISES • WASHINGTON

2001

Library of Congress Cataloging-in-Publication Data

Berg, Stephen.
Footnotes to an unfinished poem / Stephen Berg.
p. cm.
ISBN 00914061-82-8 (pbk. : alk. Paper)
I.Title

PS3552.E7 F66 2000
813'.54 –dc21

00-021880

Manufactured in the United States of America

Orchises Press
P.O. Box 20602
Alexandria
Virginia
22320-1602

G6E4C2A

CONTENTS

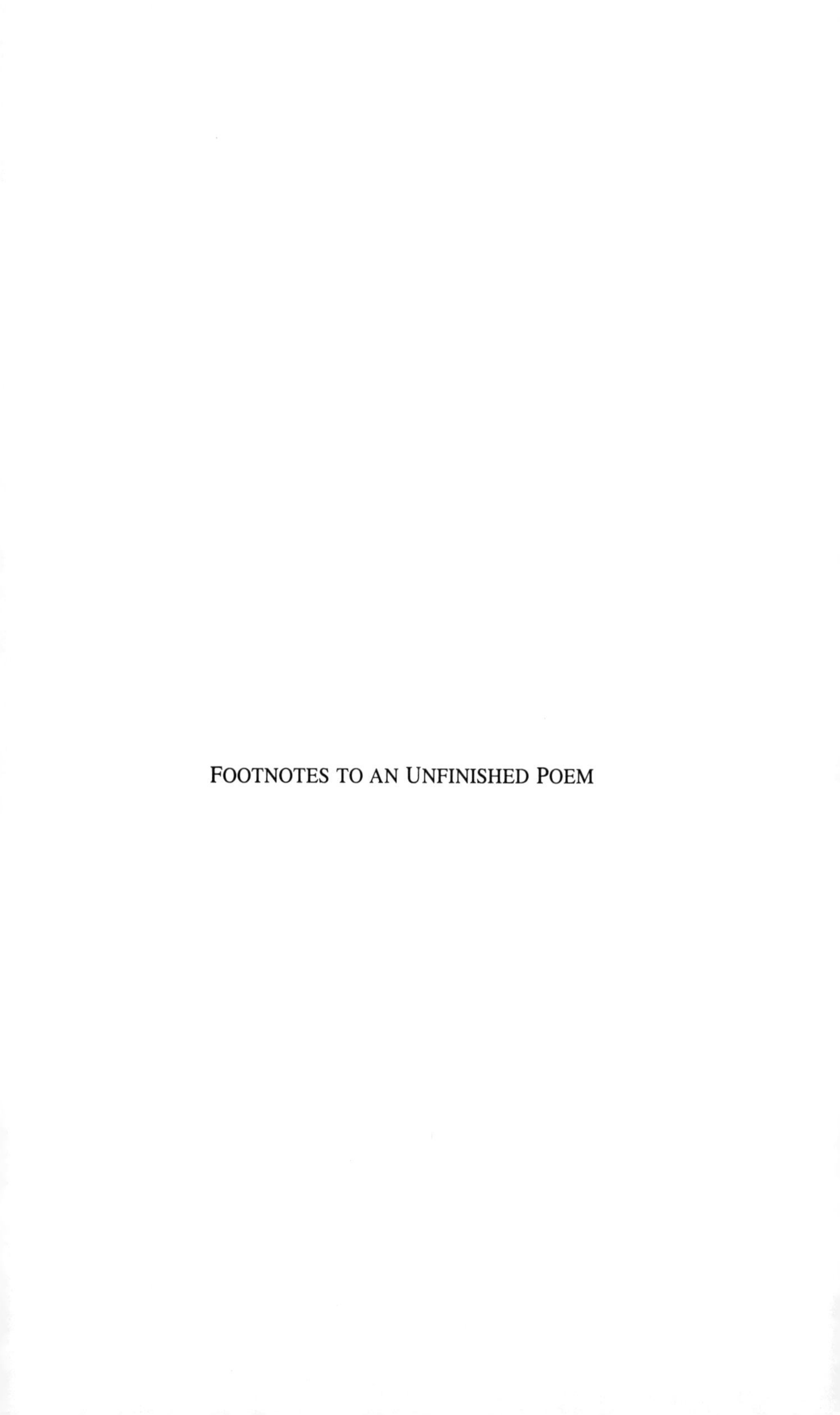

Footnotes to an Unfinished Poem

TO THE READER

Despite the apparently inadvertent comic tone of this little primer, it is a quest vision, a map of clues pointing to "the holy grail." Like all maps, it guides the reader through many places to a destination. Perhaps he or she will find some of those places as hospitable as the so-called destination.

To this author, footnotes in other books have often seemed more useful than the pages they attend. For one thing, they establish a distance from autobiography. They seem to float apart in a greater, more objective reality than our own, like stars or flowers that give themselves to the world without reservation.

The unfinished poem quoted in these pages is quasi-fiction, as are most of the footnotes. Somehow this compositional galaxy came together in random sequences—which form an aspiration, a direction, a partial unity—references to a text that its unnamed author could only fractionally complete.

The author sometimes sees his book as a mutilation of desire, drastic cosmetic surgery performed on an absent face. No real people with names, just the residue of an amputation, like phantom pain. No factual places, although a few place names occur. An "argument space," rather than an actual situation, though human interaction occurs. Something like an antidote to our inane yearning; holes punched into the silence of our ignorance; a ladder of audible, hopeless rungs.

Weil's "salvation is consenting to die" might work as an overall footnote to these footnotes, indicating the aim of its pilgrimage. In other words, perhaps the book's allegorical couple believes that to enact this quotation in their own way is to possess the grail. And yet, so many other brilliant, seductive quotes suggest themselves as methods of distilling what *Footnotes* attempts.

Throughout the process of reading and rereading the galleys for typos and revisions there were times when I thought I had almost put my hands around, seen—within myself? outside myself?—an extremely precious thing, but it turned out merely to be one more humiliation, a joke, that began with an ellipsis, a non-origin, and ended on a footnote to a footnote, a note of raw fish.

—SB

PART ONE

1. Cf. Hegel's "167. With self-consciousness, then, we have therefore entered the native realm of truth," and "...vanishing essences...." Both in *Phenomenology of Spirit.*

2. Fromm: "...desire for another person's growth."

3. "What can be described can happen too:..." begins the great finale of Wittgenstein's *Tractatus*. Those last few pages (6.362 to 6.54) may well constitute one of the most poignant, original lyric poems of this century.

4. In this stanza, I have tried to represent the meaning of the word "soul" in terms that might be acceptable to a reader wholly disinterested in religious matters.

5. "Cleansed of all resistance to reality." Erik Erikson's definition of mental health. Used here to point out EE's failure to define the place of religion in human experience.

6. "Perfect joy excludes even the very feeling of joy, for in the soul filled by the object no corner is left for saying 'I'." The sentence is from "The Self" in Simone Weil's *Gravity and Grace.* At this point in the poem it refers to those non-sexual moments of attention when time is quelled by a task that absorbs the feature of consciousness that is normally aware of our inevitable death.

7. "...this lone brightness without fixed shape or form..."quoted from p.23, Watson trans. Lin-chi in section 11 is presenting his views on the futility of seeking, on faith in oneself as the key to progress in Zen practice. The poem clearly describes a long period in the author's life when self-doubt was his primary state.

8. Porch of working-class house where his mother grew up.

9. Authentic: *Authenteo:* to have full power over; also, to commit murder. *Authentes:* not only a master and a doer, but also a perpetrator, a murderer, even a self-murderer, a suicide. Ancient denotations. Multiple references here to Greek tragedy, psychoanalytic theory (particularly Bion), Ta-Hui's Zen, Eumenides (where impersonal, cosmic forces enact themselves). This would correspond to Winnicott's comments on the full use of self in such works as late Beethoven Quartets. (See D.W. Winnicott, *Human Nature*, "The Depressive Position.")

10. Sunsets along Kelly Drive on the Schuylkill River have been noted for their beauty. *Sleeping Woman,* a public art project consisting of words running along the river's edge on top of the stone retaining wall, is installed there. It begins, "how can you know what it means to be here in the clear silence without need...." A considerable portion of wall where the line of words begins collapsed into the river a few months after the line had been stenciled and glazed on to the site.

11. "I'll just use the rain as my raincoat."– Daito.

12. Ikkyū (15th century Japanese Zen master): "Attention means attention," in answer to a student's question. It is difficult to know exactly what Ikkyū means by this. It was spoken irritably after the student refused to accept "Attention" as the answer to her question: "What is Zen?" Perhaps Ikkyū meant that attention, true attention, is like a table or chair: it has no object; it is itself.

PART TWO

1.The lovers in the poem (52 year old man, 19 year old woman) continue in their difficult situation despite all odds. Therefore the reference to Dante's Canto XVIII.

2. "Death's enormous nearness," from Emily Dickinson poem. Used here to indicate a form of attention akin to Heraclitus: "What the waking see is death." I.e. in the context of the poem, the revelatory nature of certain experiences in love allows death's constant presence to give the world a luminous, numinous aura, and makes the miracle of existence manifest.

3. Kierkegaard: here S. K. is quoted (from *Philosophical Fragments)* because he is comparing the Socratic method to the passage of time instant by instant. Cf. in the *Cratylus,* Socrates' definition of wisdom as "touching the motion or stream of things," and "the soul which is good for anything follows the motion of things, neither anticipating them nor falling behind them…" The state of mind of the lovers at this point may correspond somewhat to this condition. Cf. In *Hello, I Must Be Going,* a biography of Groucho Marx: Interviewer: "What would you do if you had your life to live over?" (Groucho is 83 at the time). Groucho: "I'd try more positions."

4. Although accentual-syllabic blank verse is the meter, prose is sometimes used, as in this portion, quoted from the novella *I Heard Jesus*. In the book, the speaker is describing an episode in a Baptist church: his over-whelming emotional response to the minister's definition of Jesus: "The One who accepts you as you are." Obviously, this occurs at times of stress between the lovers and offers them glimpses of a power that awes them.

5. "If anything exists, it is incomprehensible." Gorgias of Leontini, "On Nature." Cf. To the Zen koan "Why is a white horse not a horse?"

6. Her vagina here compared to Alfred Jarry's room, where the ceiling was so low someone of average height would have to bend over to stand in it.

7. Comparison here is to Woody Allen's habit of self-deprecation. See Wittgenstein's confession of failure in the Preface to *Philosophical Investigations,* where he calls his work of 16 years "sketches of landscapes," "only an album."

8. "Imponderable evidence includes subtleties of glance, of gesture, of tone." L. W., *Philosophical Investigations.*

9. Or "Her short black V of hair shone in the darkness,/ But nothing ever came of what she cried."

10. "Adhesive Love (Philotes)." Empedocles of Acragas, about 450 B.C., or "The animal needing something knows how much it needs, the man does not." Leucippus of Abdera, about 430 B.C. Both quotations occur, modified to fit the poem, as instructive bits of memory in the minds of both characters.

11. Although this 70-page poem tells the story of two mythical people who find a love that saves them from the hell of isolation, it would be impossible to believe in their experience as a paradigm. Not everyone will cut his arm off and offer it to Buddha for the privilege of sitting at his feet.

12. *Shtup* is used here because the music of the Yiddish far exceeds in expressiveness the wantonly used Anglo Saxon equivalent. This proves once again that the Jews possess a

more sensitive ear for the correspondences between the act and how it feels, sounds.

13. Albert Einstein and Woody Allen: comparable geniuses and shleppers.

14. How Simone Weil might have dressed if she had slept with men and changed her eating habits.

15. Jogging and biking: activities fraught with endorphine-induced insights.

16. In this bedroom scene, the prayer they say together after making love is impossible to translate into English.

17. "Love" as it appears in *Oedipus at Colonus:* the one thing that makes his and his daughters' ordeal bearable. O's abrupt, silent, painless vanishing into the underworld can be seen as redemption only if Christ's resurrection is taken literally.

18. "cunnilingus/blindness"—a most appropriate rhyme, given the scene in this passage.

19. They both actually saw His Face as a glowing bagel at the same moment. Entry in her unpublished diary.

20. Their hotel room window overlooked a large public square in Boston surrounded by apartment buildings inhabited, primarily, by Jews in business or medicine. Thus the reference to *Torah*, or "learning."

21. *Sara Lee:* the name of an expensive commercial cheesecake. The comparison here may seem exaggerated, but, on that particular night, that's how it tasted.

22. In the dark, with pink sunset light flooding the room, they did look "like raspberries."

23.The poem's shift in perspective ushers in one of the three main themes: erotic love, immortality of the soul, justice (as a term that necessarily includes religious experience as part of its meaning).

24. The phrase appears in one of the most humane stories in Western fiction, Chekhov's "Gooseberries":

I saw a happy man, one whose cherished dream had so obviously come true, who had attained his goal in life, who had got what he wanted, who was satisfied with his lot and with himself. For some reason an element of sadness had always mingled with my thoughts of human happiness, and now at the sight of a happy man I was assailed by an oppressive feeling bordering on despair. It weighed on me particularly at night. A bed was made up for me in a room next to my brother's bedroom, and I could hear that he was wakeful, and that he would get up again and again, go to the plate of gooseberries and eat one after another. I said to myself: how many contented, happy people there really are! What an overwhelming force they are! Look at life: the insolence and idleness of the strong, the ignorance and brutishness of the weak, horrible poverty everywhere, overcrowding, degeneration, drunkenness, hypocrisy, lying. Yet in all the houses and on all the streets there is peace and quiet; and of the fifty thousand people who live in our town there is not one who would cry out, who would vent his indignation aloud. We see the people who go to market, eat by day, sleep by night, who babble nonsense, marry, grow old, good-naturedly drag their dead to the cemetery, but we do not see or hear those who suffer, and what is terrible goes on somewhere behind the scenes. Everything is peaceful and quiet and only mute statistics protest: so many people gone out of their minds, so many gallons of vodka drunk, so many children dead from malnutrition. And such a state of things is evidently necessary; obviously the happy man is at his ease only because the unhappy ones bear their burdens in silence, and if there were not this silence, happiness would be impossible. It is a general hypnosis. Behind the door of every contented, happy man there ought to be someone standing with a little hammer and continually reminding him with a knock that there are unhappy people, that however happy he may be, life will sooner or later show him its claws, and trouble will come to him—illness, poverty, losses, and then no one will see or hear him, just as now he neither sees nor hears others. But there is no man with a hammer.

25. "Pang of indecision…cut deep as the bone…hope gone…like stone knocked against stone…his mind felt like an ancient temple ruin." Fragments from Egyptian poem, 1st Kingdom.

26. "The man who has become really desperate, who no longer expects anything from the world of phenomena, is flooded by the perfect joy which at last he ceases to oppose." Chapter "Obedience to the Nature of Things," in Benoit's *The Supreme Doctrine*. Ref. is to the diary of a 24-year-old whose tank was destroyed in Desert Storm, walked 5 days in desert, on 5th day he decided he was going to die. The diary says: "Once I was sure I would die and gave in to it, I accepted myself completely. I feel indestructible now."

27. "So, if I dreame I have you, I have you." From Donne's "Elegy X." Used here for love of the emotional delicacy of tone.

28. Political undercurrent of the poem: "...for between man and man the maieutic relationship is highest, and begetting belongs to God alone." One of those unattainable ideals that tortures citizens whose sense of justice and fair play cannot accept the Capitalist system.

29. Description of "rehearsal dinner" the night before wedding and amnesia caused by drinking on an empty stomach. So-called victim of "Raped and battered words" at the hands of Jewish relative refuses to quote those words. Typical of his moral position, which survives by condemnation and mystification.

30. "In the Socratic view each individual is his own center, and the entire world centers in him, because his self-knowledge is a knowledge of God." Kierkegaard in *Philosophical Fragments.* In this section of the poem, they are talking in bed one night after sex. The meticulous description of their love-making, including a few harmless perversions—the pink ribbon, cucumber, spanking—is necessary to embody, symbolically, the religious implications intrinsic to their love.

31. "And faith is what is needed by my heart, my soul, not my speculative intelligence. For it is my soul with its passions, as it were, with its flesh and blood, that has to be saved, not my abstract mind. Perhaps we can say: Only love can believe The Resurrection. Or: is it love that believes The Resurrection? We might say: Redeeming love believes even The Resurrection; holds fast even to The Resurrection." Wittgenstein, *Letters*.

PART THREE

1."...lining of the world." Milosz's term for the metaphysical realm, the side of the world God sees and we will see after death. Any true Jew thinks immediately of Bemberg Rayon, expensive material used to line jackets, and stops there. Milosz's Catholicism demands a deeper meaning. Touching, though, to imagine that behind what we see, on the "other side" of it, is something invisible to us from this side, something just as interesting and real. The male voice in the poem finds the same pleasure on this side.

2. "When I am nothing, my worth begins." From *Oedipus at Colonus;* what James Hillman calls "anima country." At this juncture, the poem's mythological intent surfaces, the latent sacred content begins to emerge. One example: "...lips like a ripe, split peach." Or the end of Lawrence's poem, "The Breath of Life": ". . . and see nothing."

3. "*Ar dapolo en strumit, tyara poon*"—as the poem progresses strange attempts at musical expression stripped of imagery or intellect explode and are allowed into the poem. More like code than nonsense. Echoes of recognizable sense remain. At this precise moment, they are praying to a dish of fruit in a hotel room: apples, grapes, oranges, pears. Cf. Delphic sacrifices and orgies: goat horns, sheep pussy, wine-soaked slave testicles. Their prayer's salacious overtones are undeniable. Curse? Aphrodisiac?

4. As they begin to experience more frequent hints of some sacred ingredient in all things, their sexual antics increase in intensity. Apparently, they believe one causes the other—both ways.

5. Name of a minor crater on the moon.

6. "Oedipus transmits the power of blessing by surrender to his weakness." Hillman, *Oedipus Revisited.* "I come to give you something, and the gift/Is my own beaten self." *Oedipus at Colonus,* Fitzgerald trans. The lovers often sit naked staring at each others' genitals for hours in the belief that such practice will trigger an epiphany.

7. "…tears from the eyes bathed the buttocks at the cleft," Canto XX, Inferno, Dante.

8. Manto. *Ibid.*

9. Belching noises.

10. The name of a fabulous beast with two mouths.

11. Believable, but usually only possible when executed by trained acrobats. The couple sometimes dreams the same dream.

12. A defense mechanism very often found in Asian women. It prevents full clitoral participation and therefore reduces greatly the possibility of mystical visions, such as this one. Details of hair and sky, anus and ears accurately portray the chaotic nature of the vision. Yes, "shaped like a jet," is appropriate. Skunk stink and sow grunts. The cripple in the vision was, in fact, wearing a green yarmulkah. The cab driver wore a silk top hat. God did have Dennis Hopper's voice and Jack Nicholson's smile. The swimming pool behind God's estate was shaped like a human penis. Mind was a duplicate of Debbie Reynolds'. No interpretations of these details are given in the poem. After this experience, they jogged 4 miles.

13. The poem now grows abstract for awhile, defining the meaning of the vision. “Snark,” “plang,” “wapple”—new religious terms, akin to “faith,” “salvation,” etc.

14. Sartre had a name for people who believed the universe was interested in them: *pigs*.

15. Same temperature as an armpit.

16. Grass the color of a green cooking apple. He was told this by an experienced but demented gardener.

17. Size of his.

18. A special need of hers.

19. Street in Vienna, where this herb could be purchased in Freud’s time. Reference is to the dangers of transference in human affairs and the near-impossibility of avoiding it. At certain times, relaxed, visible, it looks like a wild iris. Overlapping images.

20. Sound of a deer farting: rarely heard by hunters or rabbis.

21. An obsessive fantasy common to Mid-westerners, male or female. Incurable.

22. Jew vs. Gentile theme is inescapable. “Money/pussy” rhyme in these two lines is forgivable, I hope, because of the context.

23. The character’s theory in these lines is that if one treats other people the way St. Francis dealt with his “little bird sisters,” love would flood the world. He admonished them to thank God for what they had—freedom to fly, layers of feathers, food, song, spring water, mountains, hills and

rocks for shelter, tall trees—to be "grateful always." The characters hope to achieve this attitude, but fail again and again. The key word here is "humiliation," and the difficulty of availing oneself of its ever-present reality.

24. She would smear it with raspberry jam.

25. Another word for "*satori*," often experienced but rarely recognized as such because it seems so ordinary. Like seeing only what's here.

26. They look exactly like the gouges and scratches left by human fingernails on the walls and ceilings of the gas chambers.

27. Chopped chicken liver was also served. Stern Rabbinical stance.

PART FOUR

1. A portion taken from the opening of novella, *I Heard Jesus:* "These are facts I want to write down, this is about hearing Jesus, and seeing Him, briefly, like a white light staring right through my mind, seeing me and loving me. I hesitate to tell it, but I guess I want to see if I believe it myself, and the only way is to write about it. I was at the end of my life, I felt, ready to die that day when, without even thinking, I walked into the Baptist church on 17th Street under the banner that announced noon service. The church was brown everywhere inside—brown stone walls, brown wooden benches. About 30 people were sitting inside, scattered, separate. I slipped into one of the back rows right behind a black woman, who was crying a little. A man, the minister, appeared at the front, holding the Bible. He wore a nondescript gray suit and tie, nothing that would single him out. On his left a young female singer and a man were sitting at a piano.

"That was how it looked. That was where I had my 'religious experience,' if that's really what it was. I'm not sure what it was. I don't want to believe in it, hold onto it, unless I have no choice, unless it continues to affect me. And yet something in my despair wants to believe in it. I don't mind the doubt that returns me to the suffering before I entered the church. It isn't the suffering that confuses me. There will always be the suffering.

But does that moment of vision mean I see things differently now? Do any of us have the right to think he has actually heard or seen Jesus? Has my life changed since that unexpected event?"

2. "...emotions that form the substratum of our being."—T. S. Eliot, from "The Music of Poetry." Eliot

designates this as the region of consciousness any good poem will stir up and bring to the surface.

3. Dream of a murder. Nail file lost then found under a sofa pillow. Half-smoked cigarette resting on windowsill. Male and female figures. Hallucinatory remnants of a crime.

4. Fragments of a dream from same night: extremely tall young girl is swung up in the air. Glimpses of her crotch. Someone says there's a pill to make her grow up much faster. Male laughter. Guilt. Punishment in the air. Dreamer thinks it's about aggression that may explode into violence. "Nose/prose" and "fortuitous /delicious" rhymes assert the dreamer's fear.

5. Eliot, again, on music: these 9 lines attempt to use a kind of prose blank verse to prove that Eliot's position in his little-known essay, "The Borderline of Prose," fails to consider the opportunities of overlapping forms.

6. "God is, by definition, without dimension…" from final chapter of *Faustroll,* "Concerning the Surface of God," Alfred Jarry. Fleeting visions, or speculations, concerning the existence of God occur in this narrative either during fellatio or split-seconds before orgasm. It would seem to be a male phenomenon.

7. *Satori* as disaster, destruction of "old life." Destruction of beliefs=emergence of faith. "My perfect joy awaits me in the total annihilation of my hopes." Benoit once more. The sudden stretch of trochees is a deliberate reference to Lear's terrifying repetition of the single word that eliminates all events in time.

8. "pus/use"–a disturbing rhyme, given the bucolic backdrop to the incident described. The season is late spring.

9. The squirrel here is used symbolically: "It is when man sees himself as a squirrel turning round and round in a circular cage that, if he does not lie to himself, he is close to salvation." Weil, *The Mysticism of Work.* In the poem's structure, chores like dishwashing, folding napkins, waxing floors, ironing, represent spiritual activity even though they are not recognized as such by the characters.

10. Waxed drover's coat, Bergdorf Goodman version. Useless in rain. Not unlike Kafka's "The possibility of serving with all one's heart." The plot's development allows for such associations because the couple have a special gift for imagining the various modes of spiritual contact. Cf. Wordsworth's famed "meanest flower that blows."

11. "Men who shun death pursue it." Leucippus of Abdera, 203. Applies to her idea that he should be able to do it until he falls asleep, switch to tongue, fingers, toes if need be. Her perverse desire for the "pink ribbon trick" stirs his soul, not to mention his penis. Her innocent, willing sexuality gives him hard-ons instantly.

12. Reference to shamanistic pre-ecstatic euphoria as root of lyric poetry. Precedents abound, primarily in the form of denying the impermeability of the first person. Harold Brodkey's offhand pronouncement is relevant here, where the couple disappears into their perceptions of landscape: "A true 'I' is unbearable."

13. "...the stark advantages of snow." Third word in phrase chosen for its resemblance to the aural feel deep snow has, just after it has stopped falling.

14. LW's belief that one must move "from explanation to description" again and again in order to be expressively compelling is one way of justifying the poem's constant

return to situational imagery, the "where" of experience, even though this man and woman often seem detached from their environment like the mythological gods they seem to represent. Her view of things may be seen in Spenser's "of all Gods werkes, who do this world adorne,/ There is no one more faire and excellent,/ Then is mans body both for powre and forme,/Whiles it is kept in sober government." And "I saw him kisse, I saw him her embrace,/ I saw him sleepe with her all night his fill." Perhaps the whole poem's meaning-tone is condensed in Spenser's "For love is free, and led with selfe delight." They do seem tireless in their "scryne."

15. Japanese tea masters often use this crude instrument for scraping soot off the sides of the fire pit.

16. One of many such obsessions displayed in their relationship.

17. From 4th great chorus in *Oedipus Tyrannus.* Refers to mutilated eyeballs.

18. As wet and pungent as grass after a hard rain.

19. In this position he can see it clearly.

20. As in "Kiss my ass!" The usage here is the opposite of the hostile idiom. However, her following tirade suggests another level of feeling is at work. In bed, early that morning, the disruption of a bus, screaming neighbors, vandals jimmying a car door, may have caused her sensitivity to the particular act described in this passage. In Egypt's 2nd Kingdom, among royalty, it was considered normal.

21. Since the poem is set primarily in one room inside their heads in an imaginary domain, there is no reason to

believe they would have known about Tonkin Gulf. Even on her tiny porch there was enough room to perform it; the comic detail of him hanging his legs over the edge is factual. She refused. He did use her armpits in this manner and with great relish.

22. Misunderstanding as a result of her accent.

23. "Then, however, the writing of an autobiography would be a great joy because it would move along as easily as the writing down of dreams..." Kafka's *Diaries.* This nonsequitur coming from him at just that moment shows how the quality of their intimacy allowed for nonsense and blurs the distinction between gods and men.

24. To prove that any "picture" of the self is useless. This knowledge frees them.

25. These two lines try to imitate the rhythm of the act. Very difficult considering individual variations. "Like warm mango" is exactly right, for the texture and odor.

26. Rare, even among devoutly religious people, but what matters is the intensity of belief in its authenticity long after the event. To have seen such a thing unbidden!

27. As long and hard as a Zulu warrior's: reference is to *National Geographic* photograph.

28. "Dread is the possibility of freedom." Which is why, perhaps, Kierkegaard could never bring himself to do anything but write and haunt the opera houses at night. His hump is no excuse, not to this author. *Either/Or* might just as easily have been *Either/And.* As a pre-Freudian thinker, he was spared the ambivalence at the root of his decision. Nevertheless, he remains a seminal presence behind this long lyric whose strongest literary influence is the Coptic

Gospel According to Thomas, unearthed in 1945.

29. The conversion of the *Eumenides* into "bringers of good." A momentous event at the time. Murdered parental figures are found in most cults, even these days—on church walls and the walls of expensive delicatessens.

only the listener here
stricken with these crimes
silent in the silence of time's
godless

flow
like wind
licking the sacred floor

in the insatiable dream
of live

a ghost haunts
this dire parable
here here

30. She would welcome it even while reading, and continue to read. Like the wail of certain small, wild animals. There was no need to cover the floor with anything that night. Difficult but possible on their sofa. The only way to provide access at that angle.

31. They both thought Groucho's posture was caused by an unconscious fantasy—to kiss women on the navel? TV broken. Description of sky based on Dante's in *Purgatorio,* Canto III. Sudden juxtaposition: only method possible here.

32. The church he entered. Oval shape of windows. Minister's pale blue tie. These sketchy details are left deliberately incomplete in order to convey his mood

listening to the minister's words. Later, he would tell her about this, and she would connect it to her vagina, as usual.

33. French for "soreness."

34. Rimbaud and Verlaine were notorious for the same muscular innovation. *Les Illuminations* lists it, and Wallace Stevens has a version of it in his poem "The Beginning": "dewy hair." The other image here extols the use of index and middle fingers, from behind.

35. The poem now turns in the direction of higher conscious aspiration, invoking the possibilities of transcendence, or re-discovery of what Blanchot calls the "pre-original anonymous." Very similar to Zen invocation of "shitstick."

36. "O my only light . . . " George Herbert, in gratitude to God. As she quotes this, a car backfires below their window. Both mistake it for a sign, and kneel.

37. "The terrible uncertainty of my inner existence." Kafka again. Could be a footnote citing the result of his sexual failure. Such remarks are quoted in this poem as jokes. The couple cares about nothing but pleasure. They decided long ago that the tragic side of life, the thinking side that creates fear, must be dealt constant blows by any antidote that works. Another example: "Non-folly is to stand like a beggar before the threshold, to one side of the entrance, to rot and collapse." This remark of K.'s they find hilarious. Their entire adventure is dedicated to the obliteration of theory and introspection.

38. Paradoxical intention. Her taste and vocal grain: bases of devotion. Another proof of capitalism's war on erotic love.

39. Zen's basic opposition to the Socratic method. "*Mu*," for example, is a device for experiencing oneself as no more substantial than a passing sound.

40. "I am here." Milosz, from his great short chapter, "My Intention." Quoted as one of many glosses on the poem's title: HERE.

41. "Like a fireman's hat." Her answer to his question. Odd image, given her obsession with sucking on it.

42. "She kneeled above his face on the dark floor,/ Lowering herself until it filled her mouth." Here, she is facing in the direction of his feet. The verb with religious connotations in the first line helps to fulfill the poem's intention, although gods or not they always did what they did for its own sake.

43. The reference, again in the service of the couples' quest for spiritual reality, is to the last sentence in Salinger's "Franny": "Her lips began to move, forming soundless words, and they continued to move." That day they read the story aloud. Franny's fascination with the prayer: "Lord Jesus Christ, have mercy on me," her possession by it, her initiation into the community of human suffering (though she is unaware of the source of her agony), impress them greatly. Who knows what they ordered at dinner that night under the story's influence?

44. "...nature's bonfire burns on." Quoted in the poem because both of them agree that to live as Hopkins' poetry tries to inspire life in the reader's mind might well bring them closer to mystical union. The "Heraclitean Fire" and "comfort of The Resurrection" in the title fuse in their minds as phrases which suggest the third term that is the "still point," the moment in which self and universe "see"

each other, so to speak. This brand of madness haunts them. But what about Hopkins' horror at the life of the poor in Liverpool? We should find a way to combine all this, footnote by footnote, line by line, until it transfigures our love of money into a symbol for the kingdom of God. Their madness infects me! "Is immortal diamond," the Hopkins poem ends. Fitting image for their thirst. And mine.

45. "There lives the dearest freshness deep down things;" their favorite line of his, as well as "...and with bright wings." Of course, they tend to translate his passion into the sexual realm, the very contradiction that tore him apart. His crucifixion and theirs: they resolve it by accepting both.

46. "I feel a little like a clock that tells the right time,/ with the minute hand missing." Metrically aberrant lines that express her happiness, her hunch that she has already entered a new stage of energy. Cf. "Do not trouble the course of life." (Zen quote).

47. "Before falling asleep felt on my body/The weight of my fists on my light arms." This Kafka entry, turned into a near-pentameter couplet, is typical of his mind in full concentration.

48. "...he has become a spiritual worker." From Hegel's "Religion in the Form of Art." Hard not to apply this to various kinds of "work." Shape of her mouth in darkness, light of her eyes. As if she contained a source of light other than her own body. Perception described here suggests again a new phase of psychic development and a stage in the poem that promises epiphany, however doubtful.

49. "No, no, no, no, no." His mother's refusal to eat in the last stage of her illness; morphine drip. "I lifted a slice of

orange to her lips / But all she wanted was to die...." Memories of death inspire the erotic imagination, the flesh seethes with desire, with a hunger for truth.

50. "What a sober man has on his lung, a drunk man has on his tongue." His shrink's translation of Yiddish saying.

51. "You get to see God." Salinger's Franny again, explaining to her numbskull boyfriend what happens if you repeat the Jesus Prayer enough times. I suppose the author had no choice in writing the poem because of his need to find evidence of any kind for such yearning, even in fictional form.

52. "We want everything which has a value to be eternal. Now everything which has a value is the product of a meeting, lasts throughout this meeting and ceases when those things which met are separated. That is the central idea of Buddhism (the thought of Heraclitus). It leads straight to God." Weil's essay "Chance" offers this gloss. In the poem, whose story occurs in a single day, they know the terror of this idea.

PART FIVE

1. "It would be enough / If we were ever, just once, at the middle, fixed / In This Beautiful World Of Ours and not as now, / (stanza break) Helplessly at the edge, enough to be / Complete, because at the middle, if only in sense, / And in that enormous sense, merely enjoy." One of Stevens' greatest definitions of a version of what our pair of insatiable friends keeps trying to find, keeps pounding at each other to yield. Secular renditions of the experience riddle modern literature, but few accounts of the actual experience are available. The poem, although it may never be published, reports in its crippled way such an event in the author's life through two invented characters. Baldwin's "Each of us, helplessly and forever, contains the other..." applies to the form the poem was to take.

2. Nickname of Hitler's dog.

3. In the film *Viva Zapata,* Brando has his eyes taped into slits. He plays the film with almost no expression on his face. The middle-class woman he marries, played by Jean Peters, learns to make perfect tortillas and walk barefoot.

4. This description refers to the long-standing belief that in coma spiritual realities appear that resemble "withdrawing the spoke," or the new sense of time and physical existence that is inclusive in Zen thinking. Not blindness vs. sight. Standing together naked in the window, they seem as transparent (to themselves) as the glass they look through. Another Yiddish word for erection, from the saying: "When the prick goes up, the brains dive into the earth." In her case, the manifestation resembles "divine saliva," according to the phrase in the poem.

5. This unfinished poem is somewhat misnamed: although never fully composed, notes for it, phrases from it, and—difficult to pin this down—something like a damaged blueprint of it exists in the author's mind. Imagine pages of a musical composition, parts of which have been burned, erased, cut away by an insane publisher, leaving only enough clues to make these notes. Or think of it like this: instead of a whole poem, these notes upon which to imagine it. "We say ourselves in syllables that rise/From the floor, rising in speech we do not speak." Another way of saying it (from Stevens' "The Creations of Sound"). Or: a form whose pressure opens the third eye.

6. Neither above nor below. Revelation as equality.

7. Sappho's reputation for passion rests on descriptions of internal states, but also on her capacity for self-detachment and self-criticism. Ref. is to the mystical drink paralleled by the drink of cool water that is so important in Orphic afterlife scenes. Try to imagine similar libations today. *Coke? Pepsi?* Vodka martini? *Snapple?*

8. As in the vileness of a desperation so humiliating that nothing is left except the bare word "God." Faithless belief.

9. They ate shrimp scampi, escarole; veal chops, spaghetti marinara. Cheap Chianti. Meal did not impede renewed quest for salvation via 69, etc. *Alka Seltzer.* Rhyme unintended in that couplet.

10. Grandeur of one's own death, unrecognized while alive and looking forward to a good dinner. Reference to the *zzzzzzzz* of most contemporary poetry. Dull ideas, bourgeoise manners, corny metaphysics. These lines refer to a memory of near-drowning at summer camp. Ear infection, sadistic counselor. Falling in love with tennis

instructor. Her white shorts and glimpses of dark frizzy hair there. Even at that age.

11. Outside the tent, the noise of a leaky spigot. Captured in the "r" and "sh" sounds of this line.

12. Quoted from R. Maven, classics scholar, rare book dealer and master of the postcard. The "Irene" reference is to the author's dead mother, who, in Maven's opinion, has been transformed into a watchful goddess.

13. Appetite: i.e. emptiness experienced somatically in that region, and as a phallic stimulant. The erotic equivalent in Christian mysticism is undeniable, especially during PMS.

14. Harbinger, like a vision of black garter belt and black silk stockings. He has been waiting for this. Dream corresponded to promise of belt and stockings, no panties. Seven lines mix the two realities to move narrative forward, once again suggesting that redemption enters by the same door.

15. American Baptist Jewish Restaurant, the only one in continental US. Where they usually ate when not at prayer, or otherwise, in their hallucinatory room.

16. Ref. to his mother's habit of rejection and humiliation. Family's morbid atmosphere. That his uncle (on mother's side) saw doctors as Nazis and died of cancer plagued the family's view of things. Death, death, death—what wasn't a sign of death?

17. Ancient Greek for Chicken Noodle Soup.

18. She was always astonished by its size. Source of great happiness. Therefore the richness of diction and lack of caesura in this line.

19. Cf. the "wax" in Dante XVIII, *Purgatorio.* Bees and matrix for impression received by the inclination of love. "*Poi, come 'l foco movesi in altura / per la sua forma ch'e nata salire / las dove piu in sua matera dura, / cosi l'animo preso entra in disire, / ch'e moto spiritale, e mai non posa / fin che la cosa amata il fa gioire.*" Fair to say that these lines have influenced all love poetry since they were written. Its somewhat clichéd reference to ascent as the one spiritual direction no doubt fits people's intrinsic need to "rise above" painful circumstance. The fire image, too, seems predictable. But the definition of desire as a "spiritual movement" rescues the intelligence of these lines from banality. And ah! The music. Also the restlessness and rejoicing.

20. Print of a cockatoo & jungle in many hotel rooms.

21. "...and can no longer help, and once more we are orphaned and alone. So we have to content ourselves with wisdom and speculation." Therefore, "We are in a sort of hell where we can do nothing but dream, roofed in, as it were, and cut off from heaven." Wittgenstein (from a letter) on Christ's Resurrection, its reality, the results of not believing in it, and the need for faith. References here to sausage, tuna, broccoli, mushrooms, pinot noir, and other foods may be taken to imply communion as a natural act in secular life—but I doubt it. They joke about wafers with cream cheese and nova, but their anguish exceeds their belief. Cf. Gnostic idea of the "inner life," or introspection as the Kingdom of Heaven, or the notion that all existence, literally, is The Resurrection.

22. In certain states of mind this is possible.

23. Wildness on the outskirts of Chinese cities. Dirty laundry. Unwashed dinner plates. "He is reality as it is, he

is our daily life." From Benoit: definition of the guru they seek.

24. Unimaginable, but a fact.

25. Their one-burner hot plate failed to heat up.

26. These 5 lines, a comic speculation on the afterlife, are deliberately unrhymed to effect a climate of monotone in that time and place, where one can only eat standing up.

27. "Testicle / ventricle" rhyme for the purpose of stirring up a bit of horror in the reader at the thought of such a mistake.

28. In their inescapable obsession with spiritual matters, the couple often prays in this manner, crazy as it may sound.

29. Hope as opposed to how prisoners acted in Auschwitz.

30. A relative term, depending upon one's temperament and gift for self-acceptance.

31. The window shade had a large gash in it exactly at that height.

32. "Maven / raven"—joke rhyme, obvious reference to most people, in some respects, and poor Poe.

33. This long section describing them asleep is a prelude to another turning point.

34. Battered saint, or image of legs crushed in a car wreck. The face in the dream was his father's, though it lacked a nose. Patch of hair, the usual. Omnipotent glistening natives dancing and shouting in the background. The jail

cell's cold, clammy atmosphere. Partial list of details from her dream of "initiation," as she calls it in these lines.

PART SIX

1. This "Wall between ordinary life and God" repeats the main theme of the poem, in different terms. The delusion that things as they are hide God rather than reveal, embody or contain the divinity they seek. Side order of hash browns in this restaurant scene should not be overinterpreted. Same applies to gay waiter.

2. Archaic synonym for "shaky."

3. Obscure reference to the first 2½ lines in Sappho poem: "You shall be forgotten in death because you are not a good enough poet." Woman in question may already be dead. See "Justice of Aphrodite" in Fr. 1, Anne Giacomelli, University of Calgary. Her brilliant comments on "fairest flesh" and beauty, and the god's investment of beauty in a human form.

4. Biological results of this activity are not known.

5. Here they have chosen to visit a synagogue known for the excellence of its cantor. In the mood for some Flamenco-like *kvetching.*

6. Bedrock. "All suffering which does not detach us is wasted suffering." Weil, from *Gravity and Grace.* And this incident seems perfectly innocent, neither person is harmed. Calmness prevails. Hallucinated Christ without stigmata, dressed in a blue business suit (single breasted) lasts less than a minute. His crewcut does not work as a disguise.

7. O how the mind loves immediately whatever pleases it
and acts to get what it wants, your gifts of touch smell sight
etch an image of the world inside your flesh
and the mind turns to it, feels love—

to turn like that is love—repeats itself
for pleasure, then like fire whose shuddering tongues stab upward
from stuff that makes its wild shapes possible, the captive mind
inhabits desire, whose every move is spiritual, and can't rest
until what it loves makes it rejoice. I hope you know
that those who say each love is wonderful are far
from the truth: not everything that stamps the wax is good
though the wax is. This is Truth:

— XVIII, from *Purgatorio,* author's version. It breaks off because he was unable to complete the version. Quoted here because of its relevance to their struggle, their archetypal presences in the text. Image of disheveled clothing on chairs and floor may be construed as symbols of the mind's plight: no proof of soul's immortality.

8. Reference is to cocktails after a family funeral, when someone said of the deceased: "I know he's listening to every word we say." Superstition, belief, fake piety? Difficult to tell from his tone of voice, which was always the same no matter what he said.

9. Dollar bill enclosed for some unknown reason with letter. She bought skim milk with it. Vulgarity of letter manifested in its refusal to describe what actually happened, use of vague references, injured tone, assumption of secret, superior knowledge—all causing mystification to recipient. This is typical of letter writer's culture of evasion and hypocrisy. After discussing the letter, she blew him as a consolation, which precipitated flashback of recent hallucinated Jesus.

10. Six lines of pre-Socratic philosophy on "flux," arranged in a surreal collage. Used here to support the character's assumption: "disciple of his own mind." From Silvanus. Also: "If you bring forth what is within you, what you bring forth will save you. If you do not bring

forth what is within you will destroy you." From *The Gospel According to Thomas.*

11. "To the perfect, invisible God to whom one speaks in silence—" the prayer moves into a chant of sacred words and vowels: "Zoxathazo a oo ee ooo eee oooo ee oooooooooooo oooooo uuuuuu oooooooooooo ooo Zozazoth." From Zostrianos. Questionable, this rabid ardor and its consequences. All from Pagels, *The Gnostic Gospels.*

12. Her fear of swallowing it. At first she would wash it down with a Coke. "...guided by powers wiser than I." From Milosz's *A Year of The Hunter.* Passages of deep sensitivity, and yet paucity of introspective insight somewhat strange. As if self-knowledge were forbidden to someone with such great intelligence and political wisdom. Perhaps the humility of his ambivalence balances this out. In this section of the poem, both fail to come.

13. "Shaped like a bucket that continues to glow," Dante again, from same canto in *Purgatorio.* The moon's light causes some stars to disappear from sight. No doubt elicited by the color of cream cheese on rye they ate that morning in bed. Amazing to watch gods eat!

14. Like banana cream pie.

15. Trees in that part of Boston, where there are many dogs. Dried, it is sometimes used by children for hockey pucks.

16. The fact that he thought sparrows chirping was human laughter is ominous. Possibly fatigue. Possibly the onset of another vision. The mockery of that sound: guilty hallucination.

PART SEVEN

1."The searing twilight scarred him, shook his mind," refers to the bloody streaks of cloud, fringing the treeline. See Gauguin's red trees in his painting of the crucifixion for a similar image. In such states the blood of Christ may be seen tinting any object, from *Buicks* to *Ferragamo* loafers.

2. Perfect *Oxxford* jacket and tie for the occasion. The only disappointment was the faint scent of smegma rising from one of the pockets. Spanish cloth, *Fendi* red and black silk tie.

3. Tillich's "God beyond God," in *The Courage To Be.* A constant vagueness of thought, seductive in its tendency to convince susceptible minds, like these lovers'. But you have to sympathize with their naïve, earnest hopes. After all, all they have is each other, and not even that. Heaven?

4. Style of entire poem based on postcard format. Unknown author of cards sent to ex-teacher. Background of poem's tone and diction, difficult to substantiate without quoting extensively from irrelevant, beloved correspondence, much of which is lost.

5. Poem now spins into new orbits of association. Mbyua sickness mask: twisted nose, closed left eye (white); blackish right side (open eye). Cf. Rilke's "Death always says Yes." *(Letters).*

6. The order (plot) of these footnotes fails to convey the poem's inspired, comic attempt to assuage the reader's existential pain. Camus' nostalgic, tender ironies inform this section, but, alas, that man with his sad bulging eyes is gone.

7. Japanese quality of *saba*. At times he could not stop his hands from doing it. Reflexive actions. No text can represent the human animal's need in this area—as if the flesh knows its doom and drowns in desire and tenderness. But perhaps the poem's condition—fragments, long completed portions, brief stretches still in revision, holes—captures more of this feeling than a finished poem could. Nevertheless, the author has decided not to publish it in its current state.

8. "And when I see the thick white body of train smoke break," penultimate line from Lawrence's poem "Erotic."

9. "God does not reveal himself *in* the world." (6.432, Wittgenstein's *Tractatus).* This statement is like the human skull that contains and protects the brain from the world: it is the verbal impasse to the couple in the poem. L. W. emphasizes the preposition "in" by putting it in italics, but why? Suppose he had said "through." All this reminds us of L. W.'s refusal to talk about the metaphysical, thus protecting it at the same time from attack. This is the heart of the poem—their pathetic obsession with transcendence. This is the broken heart of the poem—its failure to make sense of this realm to the extent that a reader might be moved to believe. This is why, finally, the author refuses to publish it. These notes form a kind of fence around the poem, a fence made of slats between which the reader may peek. This strategy, then, to the author at least, manifests more than the poem can of what the pair seeks that is metaphysical—by making it impossible for the reader to read the actual poem, by giving him clues to an invisible text?

10. "And it is not surprising that the deepest problems are in fact *not* problems at all." (4.003, *Ibid,* not italicized). This serious downturn in the poem probably caused by their continuing grief, whose cause remains mysterious.

The reader may be aware of same in himself, and identify with theirs.

11. Pig sounds they rehearse as responses to the last line (7) in L. W.'s *Tractatus.* They also summon up farts, whistles, guttural noises and psychotic laughter, and in these 12 lines sketch out a one-act play whose only language is those sounds, with L. W.'s last line as the play's title.

12. "...not one master is left/mind slices a hair/blown against it nothing is cut it cuts itself/ nowhere everywhere happens I hear/ the emptiness gnash its teeth"—Daito's death poem. Quoted here as a temporary resolution to their grief.

13. "Pure and ready to rise to the stars." Guess who? Quoted in the poem to underscore their distance from his accomplishment.

14. "Let X be the median extension of one of the persons a, 2y the side of the triangle to which it is perpendicular. N and P the extensions of the straight line (a + x) in both directions *ad infinitum."* A portion of Jarry's lunatic formula in the *Faustroll* chapter "Concerning the Surface of God." More likely a proof of the ego's need to rid itself of the poison of metaphysical desire. A kind of surreal orgasm. An intellectual dump.

15. "I have too much to do and too little time to do it in." From a conversation on Time with French physicist and prose poet Samuel Mack; "...make a wall of yourself," from *Purgatorio,* XXVI, recommended. After a few beers the problem dissolved. Reference to shed in Mack's yard: he compared sink hole under the floor with trying to live life "fully," and with the hope that one might stop hearing such mad questions echo again and again in one's head.

16. “I don’t want to die, I want to watch cartoons.” Child’s assertion overheard one Saturday watching TV.

17. It was a 4-button fly. First, she would rub it with both hands at once. This couplet brings together in highly condensed form the entire physical-metaphysical theme of the allegory, and the inescapable suffering caused by social pressures coupled with the limitations of mind. At least they kept trying, or was that their mistake?

18. On friend’s porch, soaked from a 20-mile bike ride to Waltham. References to dead Jewish friend’s rather large hooked nose, and the silence of his absent voice, how the world sounds different now. Friend, in his usual insightful way: “Perhaps that silence is God’s voice.” For a split second, we believed it!

19. Background Reality: a belief once held by monks in the Ming Dynasty.

20. “Tip” or “head”—interchangeable terms for that instrument’s forward part. Revered for its sensitivity to human contact. Used here as a site where spiritual sensations occur, though not usually acknowledged as such. Completely non-mental and sometimes jokingly associated with The Resurrection. Also, another kind of communion wafer.

21. The card game was poker. Laughter not theirs.

22. Fragment of an ancient Hebrew recipe, perhaps for a meat dish.

23. “A spatial point is an argument-place.” And “Objects contain the possibility of all situations.” L. W. Of course.

24. Twine used for tying roasts.

25. Usually made of plastic with small electric motor inside. Wooden ones must be carefully finished to prevent splinters. Wonderful word "vibrate."

26. Top string on Irish lyre.

27. This duet of theirs was jointly written in an attempt to create a congregation of two, as well as to entertain guests. Five-word fragment of a dirty joke at the end is actually from a 5th century Greek façade found near Paestum: "It was too big to…" is another translation.

28. Sliced thin, with mustard. Cf. *Cratylus,* "…to express the attributes of the god…." Or "Thus we have: X == ∞ —N a—P." (Jarry)

29. Matzoh.

PART EIGHT

1. "Jesus is the world's crisis."—Jaspers, *Socrates, Buddha, Confucius, Jesus.* Therefore, one experiences the crucifixion and resurrection as constant principles at work in everyday life, moment by moment, not merely as disembodied symbols: one interpretation of Jasper's meaning. In the poem, they sense this suffering presence's release, and it illuminates the world. Poem is unfinished in part because of author's failure to embody this, or to present their doubt-rotted faith with conviction.

2. That year his ex-wife dies of melanoma. Sky-blue panties. On death-bed she promises never to wear panty-hose again. Black garter belt and stockings. She inherits 900K from father. Scene depicts them behind dark glass windows of limo, celebrating, thus the bizarre imagery of imagined bodies. Infinite matrix.

3. "You were born out of me." In a dream, he hears this compliment from a stranger. Do these three lines describing a beaver swimming with a stick in its mouth toward a dam represent their new stage of conversion? Think of its miniature paddling paws. Surrounding trees seem to speak. Water is the color of rotten avocado. Clouds like morse code.

4. Now the poem is urged in a new direction by their passion. Even their dreams reflect it. Nights become a series of thresholds leading to another world, as in Kafka's "Evil does not exist; once you have crossed the threshold, all is good. Once in another world, you must hold your tongue." Possibly this statement was one of the obstacles to finishing the poem. It echoes, too, the fearsome dictate of silence that ends Wittgenstein's *Tractatus.* When was the last time you met a Rabbi who kept his mouth shut?

5. Our author had planned to study for the Rabbinate but was sidetracked by puberty, which lasted, oh, any number of years. Now it returns in the form of religio-erotic impulses which motivate his maimed text. These lines confess as much. The reference to *Saltines* fits perfectly his humiliations as a child. Step by step from here on the poem develops the lovers' final vision, much like "It is enough that the arrows fit exactly in the wounds that they have made." (Kafka)

6. They are shaped like gefilte fish sometimes, but the taste is entirely different, obviously. Defecatory noises from behind the door, mixed with car horns and other street sounds—as they lay awake, thinking of their distance from God. Quote here is from S. Berg's "Our Ignorance," in *Congregation.* His term for this constant possibility is "disguised gods."

7. The entire poem can be seen as an answer to Kafka's "What have you done with your gift of sex?" The "noodle/hurdle" rhyme brilliantly supports this.

8. Hebrew for "fine tuning."

9. In Taiwan sleeping in this position is common.

10. "However, sincc difficulty also can be accounted for in two ways, its cause may exist not in the objects of our study but in ourselves: just as it is with bats' eyes in respect of daylight, so it is with our mental intelligence in respect of those things which are by nature most obvious." —Aristotle, *Metaphysics,* Book II. Our couple never for a moment forgets this, is plagued by this. Reference at end of stanza is to adolescent farting contests, using either the real organ or the hand-in-armpit version.

11. American painter Ralph Tooter—compared with the shape of his nose. The fire image here is based on Tooter's painting "Flame Head."

12. *Ratner's Deli,* Lower East Side, famous for its omelettes. The couple ate there once, before visiting one of the countless gurus they saw to advise them on their quest.

13. Color of poisonous snake found in Upper Silesia.

14. These cries are emitted because of her great surprise. She compares it to a small tree trunk, to his delight, and is all too willing to suffer the consequences. Mood like black snow.

15. They vow it. That's the tone.

16. Her euphemism for how it feels in her mouth. "bauble/trouble" rhyme states, musically, an essential physical characteristic contributing to her obsession with Christ's pathetic feet. Not stoical resolution but vatic mania is her state of mind when she performs this feat.

17. Reference is to her father's habit of praying outside her closed bedroom door. That fact certainly elicited his pity the first time he heard it. "Pursuit" a mere metaphor for the force compelling them. Orestes reference harrowing. Grape reference is to her "wine-soaked hem."

18. He craves that particular consistency and smell.

19. She compares what bursts from him to muscatel.

PART NINE

1. "The artificer therefore unites the two (the self both as inner and outer) by blending the natural and the self-conscious shape, and the ambiguous being which is a riddle to itself, the conscious wrestling with the unconscious, the simple inner with the multiform outer, the darkness of thought mating with the clarity of utterance, these break into the language of a profound, but scarcely intelligible wisdom." (Hegel, *Phenomenology of Spirit.)* Overwhelmingly true.

2. "The whole secret lies in arbitrariness." And "The arbitrary in oneself corresponds to the accidental in the external world." The male character has always pitied Kierkegaard for the degree of truthful intensity his mind bore, but it has given him faith, has consoled him with its bitter, noble songs. The couple is like a pair of blurred shadows at twilight in this scene, standing naked in the window, looking out over the cold dark trees, holding hands. Description of wind accurate, or "like a bodiless voice." Section from little-known masterpiece of "anonymous confession," *Porno Diva Numero Uno* may help to show what they have seen that is beyond the uses of speech:

no one ever thinks of not believing in 'I am' ridiculous to 'believe in oneself' might as well begin our next visit there dramatically because what about delay your name for the large glass this time he seemed bored distracted but he was amazing his absolute sincerity the sincerity of not being watched ever of never caring about being seen of simply being himself though that notion would have made him laugh puke since notions of self and being he detested I think but I watched him pace a bit then go up to a painting and stare for a moment pick his nose cough look out the window belch sit down get up leave the room be right back when he was gone my mind spoke continually imagining what he might say and that has crept into this from the beginning a form something profound about the way his silences and his presence suggested soliloquies in your head which would start and go on then halt shift go in any direction I'd call him Liberator like sitting with a great Maquis survivor patient though a great war raged outside silent Duchamp had fought the inner war to a standstill by an act of speechless patience detachment humor acceptance who knows what he came back into the living room one accepts everything while laughing just the same said in an interview right yes people forget how close together roles are privacy in the studio celebrity around the corner on the stage of a theatre death sex now those are two plus art that can't be on stage easily they are the real celebrities they exist only between back between again death sex art always between can't and have think about it *etants donnee* my so-called last piece is not really the last the last is one only I've seen only I know where it is and I will remain unknown invisible that's the only way to make art at this point in this world however I can discuss that work a bit if you like difficult though because of my hatred of concepts it does have a title HAND but in reality it's like a voice or a sound of some sort choral aria-like as this duet-soliloquy should be but that's not it imagine a visible voice can you voices are invisible of course but this voice my voice this last piece no one will see ever or experience at least not as my work of art is a visible voice without the presence of a speaker a machine a screen a needle think of yourself sitting down to read you move your eyes across the words left to right back again left right back and you hear many things you don't see a garbage truck footsteps birds a kid screaming you know where those voices came from you have names for the sources of the voices so even though you can't see the things emitting sounds you recognize them but my voice HAND even though it's called HAND familiar thing it does not sound like a sound a voice coming from anything or anyone you know so it's a voice without a nameable source all the voices we know have a source we know human or otherwise lines from a favorite poet whose anonymous source no one can explain define properly will give you a hint *Je suis maitre de silence* or *La musique savante manque à notre désir* or *Un Souffle ouvre des breches operadiques dans les cloisons* you can hear in those sentences the absence of the individual the presence of a voice that without personal intention or specific qualities my HAND voice is not composed of words exactly though obviously it must have a sound it's not abstract either somewhere between a voice that makes sense and a voice like the wind's unpredictable wandering especially when it's strong enough to hear clearly is what I'm saying the single hand source activates if you were to see it you would not recognize it in that sense god-like though I call it HAND but it would defeat the pleasure I get from the piece and its place among us its situation to say more about something which after all in the way I've explained really doesn't exist not even for me

3. "Whoever sustained his certainties without fail / across your naked back with the sting of a whip / is dead, Now what? Who will you blame now? Fix your eyes on the wild sky, / which never thinks and is never the same, and ask it."—ends unpublished poem by the author. That last night together, specks shaped like leaves or blurred phrases glowed in the sky. The darkness quivered as if readying to leave. All that night they said nothing and listened to each other breathe. They each sat in a lounge chair. They mumbled, dozed. Immortal moment.

4. L. 1705, *Oedipus at Colonus,* Chorus: "He lived his life."

5. Sky suddenly black, buildings black, street black.

6. "But the art of naming appears not to be concerned with imitations of this kind." *Cratylus.* Hardly different.

7. "It is a fault to wish to be understood before we have made ourselves clear to ourselves." And "The same words can be commonplace or extraordinary according to the manner in which they are spoken. And this manner depends on the depth of the region in a man's being from which they proceed without the will being able to do anything. And by a marvelous agreement they reach the

same region in him who hears them. Thus the hearer can discern, if he has any power of discernment, what is the value of the words." And "Love of God is pure when joy and suffering inspire an equal degree of gratitude." All from "Love" in *Gravity and Grace,* Weil.

8. Image of untouched *Saltines* on plate deliberately cut off from the rest of the scene, unclear. Barely alive, they sit there, stiff with fear.

9. Flashback to Christ's voice in Baptist church, noon service: "…you as you are." Detail is back of woman's sobbing head in the row in front of him. He asked her for a *Kleenex.*

10. Did he move on to easier things? Did she demand he lift his stupid bones and speak? Did He appear and cure their incomprehensible fever?

11. Impossible to tell from this draft of manuscript, since the narrative seems to break off and yet presents imagery that seems conclusive, whether the author did end it here. The fusion of national, cosmic, domestic and erotic terms suggests a desire to synthesize as much as possible at this point.

12. "This incarnation of the Divine Being, or the fact that it essentially and directly has the shape of self-consciousness, is the simple content of the absolute religion." She reads this to him in the dark and says, "Wouldn't it be great if it were written on the Goodyear Blimp?"

13. "Stars and blossoming fruit-trees: utter permanence and extreme fragility give an equal sense of eternity." Weil, from "Chance." Perfect here, in their wretched, prophetic silence.

14. In this final snapshot of baffled secrecy, we see them toast and simultaneously drink in the dark room. Gods on a frieze. Their glasses tingle with alien light. Image is of them seen from outside, as if the spectator were hovering in air ten storeys up. Gesture of hands swooped up and clapped to their mouths just before they toast, as if to swallow something. Lips. Unclear. Thin vowels of these lines try to capture breathing, unbearably slow, in unison. They still stand. One breath. Grey silhouettes.

15. Phrase describes their state—from William James' "Continuous transition is one sort of conjunctive relation; and to be a radical empiricist means to hold fast to this conjunctive relation above all others, for this is the strategic point, the position through which, if a hole be made, all the corruptions of dialectic and all the metaphysical fictions pour into our philosophy." Should we tolerate such destitute hymns, is there any way to defend ourselves against their tortured, seductive beauty? Essential here.

16. Night's delicate eyelids close
on pines and silent hills
my body dark as the darkness

A recently discovered poem by Bashō, roughly translated. The reference in the poem is to the high insight the god-like couple has at this moment: "The cheap rug seemed to glow like the red floor / Of no known house in no familiar town; / They lay there, quiet, listening to the street / Reveal secrets they never would have thought / Could save them from despair...."

17. Their *satori-orgasm*. Before it, they had been reading a series of free-meter Haiku, proofs of *satori*, by Ippekiro:

sunlight chicken head
shivering on the wall's
my dead mother's face

I would never have cut that
white peony but
I hated its beauty

how many billion skulls
are smiling right now
under my feet?

my ordinary clean hands
held open until
I have to shit

imagining death:
somebody else's kind words
finding me

or the inside of a walnut
that cannot see
it's a walnut

like the tip of a needle
death can't be seen but
near it everything seethes

woke with her warm nipple
in my mouth
dogs barking at each other

sweet delicious nova
on a toasted bagel
without onion![1]

my koan's a perfect hard-on
that won't go down
no matter how long I fuck

ants on the kitchen countertop
can't see my hand
or feel my lack of pity

even so I'd like to be
someone who lets them eat
you're not dirty

tiny Chekhovs
teaching me how
not to brush you away

time's no heavier
than one of you
crawling on my finger

These examples suggest a forgotten definition of *satori*: the discovery of one's central, personal koan—a situation in everyday life—and the realization that it cannot be solved unless it is seized as a question the instant it is first asked by someone, heard by someone else. The actual life situation embodied by these poems is only symbolically represented. *Satori* is, according to this notion, a state of suspension between question and answer, but one's mood in this state of psychic realignment is crucial: even imminent death would feel no different from receiving the bank's monthly notification of electronic deposit of one's paycheck, i.e., one would not anticipate threat or injury in either case.

18. On the wall, "white vibrant square" is a shadow-window filled with wildly crisscrossing branches. Could be one entrance to the Other Side. Voice they hear is no one's. Or is it . . . ?

19. Great relief to have come this far without encountering even a hint of Rilke's ridiculous hermaphroditic, angelic consciousness. The lovers, who know his *Elegies* well, despise the idealized consciousness of those post-heroic interpretations of their own more accessible, redemptive, mundane ordeal. Hopelessness as salvation. Cf. Bellow's "Lead me not into Penn Station."

20. "*L'animo, ch'e creato ad amar presto*," oh what a woeful source for these last crippled notes: "Night rocked them in its lap, like a blind mother,/soothing their nonexistent bodies…"

1. Jewish version of sushi, deliberately converted to that cultural equivalent here.